The Farm Five:

The Mystery of the Strange Pudding

SAMAY SRIVASTAVA

To my father

For supporting my writing journey

Contents

Meet The Farm Five

There is a farm on the edge of the Pench National Park in Northern Maharashtra. On that farm lives a farmer who loves his farm animals. He can even speak their language. He often leaves the farm animals alone because they can look after themselves. Among these animals are the world-famous "Farm Five". Each of them has special powers. They are:

- **Piggy, the pig.** Piggy's special power is that he can roll as fast as a Peregrine Falcon (the world's fastest bird) despite being round and heavy. While rolling, he crushes anything on his way, turning it into a carpet.

- **Doo, the donkey.** Doo's back kick is so strong that he can smash almost anything. He is also very passionate about singing. But his voice is so loud that it could shatter window panes, crockery, carnivores' canines, cattle horns, and even car headlights.

- **Meow, the Persian cat**. Despite being lazy, Meow is very intelligent, can use an iPad, cook delicious food and speak human languages.

- **Tandoori, the rooster**. Tandoori has an extraordinary power that he would turn into a Pteranodon (a large flying dinosaur) when someone would pull his cockscomb.

- **Alex, the Border Collie dog**. Alex is the leader of the gang. Apart from being naturally courageous, Alex has extraordinary smelling power. He also has a box of detachable noses that he could fit above his nose to increase his smelling power.

Apart from the Farm Five, there are other fascinating animals, including:

- Lamb no 77. The most intelligent sheep in the herd of one hundred.

- Naughtyhorsey. One of the naughtiest animals on the farm. He is Doo's brother and shares the stable with him.

- Pahari, the goat. Pahari is Piggy's best friend. She is half Himalayan Goreal and half domestic goat.

Since the farm is located at the edge of the jungle, the farm animals have made friends with some very peculiar jungle animals, including:

- Sherkhan, the Bengal tiger. Sherkhan is the king of the jungle.

- Ballu, the bear wizard. Ballu lives in a cave near the lake. He has many magic tricks and makes potions from rare jungle flowers and herbs. He has a crystal ball called "Google Ball" that can give any information. However, his magic tricks often go wrong, leading to funny moments.

- Ting-Tong, the craziest Cheetal deers in the entire world. Ting and Tong are twin brothers adopted by Ballu as his magic assistants.

- Dakia, the post-bunny. He delivers letters to all jungle animals.

- Dherkhan, the evil brother of Sherkhan. He has a small forest patch between the forests of Ballu and Sherkhan.

- Kallu, the evil witch. Kallu is Ballu's twin sister. She helps Dherkhan, the evil tiger. She is very bad-tempered.

- Bilota, the sly, cunning cat. He has a half-orange and half-blue skin with a peculiar long neck. He is the cousin brother of Meow, but he became a space thief and joined the evil gang of Dherkhan. He is an active member of www.earthkharabkaro.com

- Willy, an alpha male Dhole (Asiatic Wild dog) and a friend of Dherkhan. He and his pack help Dherkhan and Bilota in their evil hunting tricks.

- Lakkha, a Stripped Hyena and a friend of Dherkhan. He and his pack scavenge the kill left by Dherkhan.

- The Giggling Gang, a group of thirteen rats named— Heehee, Haha, Hoho, Giggler, Grin, Guffaw, Laugh, Cackle, Sneer, Snigger, Chuckle, Smile and Smirk. They are very notorious and irritate everyone by non-stop giggling.

Chapter 1
A Strange Email

"Yay!" said Piggy, one fine summer morning. "We solved our first advanced mystery. Did you have fun, Alex, solving the mystery of the Strange Carpenters?"

"Of course, I had fun solving the mystery of the Strange Carpenters," barked Alex, wagging his tail.

"And who would believe that those Strange Carpenters were Ting-Tong!" said Doo joining the conversation.

"Oh, I enjoyed solving the mystery of the Strange Carpenters, too," said Tandoori.

Suddenly, the kitchen door burst open, and Meow's voice was heard.

"Look! I've got a new email on my Mewpad."

The four of them trooped in to see the email.

Mewpad was Meow's special iPad. She had converted it into cat language instead of English.

"Look, here is the email," said Meow and clicked on it.

This is what it said:

Dear Farm Five,

I know that you have solved the mystery of the Strange Carpenters, and that is very, very nice. So, I am sending you a huge pudding as a reward. It will be strawberry-flavoured, so the colour will be pink.

And please share it with Naughtyhorsey, Pahari, sheep, hens, goats, cows, bulls and ducks.

Thanks. ☺

Regards,

Laboti Alluk.

PS: It will arrive tomorrow morning.

"Yummy," said Piggy.

"What a strange email" wondered Doo.

"A huge pudding," said Tandoori gleefully.

"Strawberry flavour, my favourite," said Meow.

"Who is this person called Laboti Alluk?" asked Alex thoughtfully.

"I don't know, Alex," said Meow.

"All the same, we are getting a delicious pudding," said Piggy happily.

"You always want something to eat, Piggy!" said Doo.

"Anyway, the pudding will come tomorrow," said Tandoori.

"Come, let's tell all the animals about the pudding," said Meow.

They all went out to tell the other animals about the pudding. Everyone was very excited and happy to hear about the gift.

"Very good!" said Pahadi excitedly.

"Yumm-yum-yummy," said Lamb no 77.

"Who sent this email?" asked Naughtyhorsey.

"I don't know, but who cares," replied Piggy.

That night, Piggy had dreams of the delicious strawberry pudding. "Yummy", he thought, "Yummy!"

Chapter 2
A Big Mysterious Pudding

The next day, the Farm Five were awakened by the sound of a huge truck.

"The pudding has arrived!" cried Piggy, jumping out of his bed and running out of his shed.

Sure enough, it had. A big truck stopped at the gate. From inside came out ten strong creatures carrying an enormous pudding bowl. The bowl was at least the size of a car.

The strong creatures put the pudding in the middle of the farm, returned to the truck and drove off.

"Yummy", said Piggy, rubbing his hands in glee.

All the farm animals began to come towards the pudding. Lamb no 28 ran to take a bite.

Suddenly, the pudding shook, and all the animals jumped back, startled.

"Goodness, what just happened," asked Naughtyhorsey.

Lamb, no 28, leaned over the bowl to take a bite.

Suddenly, the pudding shook violently again, and Lamb no 28 fell right into the pudding.

"Help, I am drowning," she squealed.

Doo ran to help, but 28 had already drowned. Doo put his long legs to search for 28, but the pudding shook yet again. Doo lost his balance and fell into it. He, too, got sucked in instantly.

Piggy ran to help Doo, but he also got sucked in. Sheep began to help Piggy, but they also got sucked in. Goats ran to help the sheep, but the pudding sucked them in too.

"Get back. This is a dangerous pudding," yelled Alex.

Meow ran to get a very long stick and put it inside the pudding, but that, too, disappeared.

"Good heavens," exclaimed Meow, sinking back in terror.

Suddenly, the pudding bowl jumped up and began to shoot strings of pudding that pulled in Naughtyhorsey, ducks, bulls, cows, and hens.

Alex, Meow, and Tandoori were the only ones left. The pudding began to jump towards them, and they backed away at once.

Alex saw Dakia, the post-bunny and yelled at the top of his voice.

"Dakia, quick, give Ballu my message that there is a crazy pudding bowl at the farm, and it has sucked in all the farm animals. We need his help!"

Dakia shot off.

The pudding bowl threw very long pudding strings and pulled in Meow and Tandoori. Alex was quick to sense. He dodged the pudding strings.

The collie ran towards the jungle like a deer. But the pudding bowl leapt like a cheetah and sucked him as well.

Chapter 3
Ballu Comes to Help

Dakia was very fast indeed. Before entering Ballu's cave, he peeped into Ting-Tong's cave in case they were after this mystery. However, Ting-Tong were still into carpentry. They were trying to make a bed using a rifle instead of a drilling machine, hammer and nails.

Then Dakia went into Ballu's cave.

"Good morning, sir. I have a message from Alex. He says that the farm is in danger, and you need to come to help immediately," Dakia explained the entire incident.

Ballu went pale. "I need to check about this on my Google Ball". He pressed the Google Ball and said, "Google Ball, Google Ball, googlest of all, please show me the strange pudding incident."

The Google Ball played back the entire incident. Then it showed the strange email. Ballu read it and clicked the sender's name on the email. The Google Ball reorganised the spelling from "Laboti Alluk" to "Bilota Kallu".

"Good heavens!" said Ballu in alarm.

Kallu and Bilota were Ballu's worst enemies. Kallu was Ballu's evil twin sister, and Bilota was Meow's wicked cousin. They worked for Dherkhan, the evil tiger, along with Lakhha, the hyena and Willy, the dhole. They were always trying to kill and eat the farm animals.

Ballu quickly got up and dragged his sleigh outside.

"Ting-Tong! Quick, the farm animals are in danger! Take me to the farm immediately", said Ballu.

Ting-Tong came out of their cave. Seeing Ballu in a hurry, they lifted the sleigh and began running towards the farm.

"Ting-Tong, STOP!" yelled Ballu, clinging to the sleigh for his dear life.

Ting-Tong dropped the sleigh, and Ballu fell out of it with a crash.

"Not like this, you idiots. Drag the sleigh like the reindeer drag Santa Claus and take me to the farm."

"Santa," said Ting.

"Claus," said Tong.

Then, they both began to dance and sing.

"Jingle bells, jingle bells…"

"Idiots, save animals first, then sing Christmas carols", said Ballu.

"Alright, Boss," said Ting and Tong, hastily pulling the sleigh.

They took Ballu three-fourths of a kilometre when Ting began to sing again.

"Jingle bells, jingle bells…"

"It's dashing through the Snow, not jingle bells", said Tong.

"No, it's jingle bells", said Ting indignantly.

Then, they both began to fight and started boxing each other. Tong boxed Ting so hard that Ting fell, and the sleigh crashed.

"Idiots", said Ballu as he was thrown into Piggy's pond.

Ballu got out of the pond and shook his body. Ting-Tong could not be seen anywhere. He suddenly saw the strange pudding in the middle of the farm. He quickly took out his magic wand and froze the pudding with a spell. He then lifted the pudding bowl on his head.

All of a sudden, he heard a noise from the jungle. He looked up to see Kallu, Bilota, Dherkhan, Lakha, and Willy, along with an army of hyenas and wild dogs.

"Give us that pudding, Ballu," growled Dherkhan. "I am powerful, and I have a hundred hyenas and wild dogs, and Kallu has her magic wand."

"Pooh, I am a Karate Blackbelt, and I have a powerful magic wand and a pocket Google Ball," said Ballu.

"And I have something called a gun", said Bilota with a wicked grin and to Ballu's horror, he took a real revolver out of his pocket.

"And now I shall kill you," he said.

He aimed the gun at Ballu's head and fired. "Bang!"

There was a loud bang as the bullet missed Ballu by an inch. It hit the farmer's bedroom window pane, which shattered to pieces.

Suddenly, out of nowhere came a car, knocking Ballu's enemies to the ground. A familiar voice called Ballu,

"Come on, boss, get in quick!"

Chapter 4
Ting-Tong Take Charge

"Ting-Tong!" cried Ballu in delight. He jumped in the car, opened the sunroof, and, using his magic wand, held the pudding on top.

"Off we go!" yelled Tong as Ting hit the accelerator, and the car shot off.

This was too much for Bilota. He ran and stole three bikes from the nearby farm. He gave one to Willy, one to Lakha, and took one for himself. Then they went behind Ballu and Ting-Tong.

Ting-Tong's car went down the village lane at full speed as pedestrians jumped out of the way.

Bilota fired his second bullet at the car, but Ting-Tong dodged it. The bullet hit a lamp post that fell on Willy. He got an electric shock and crashed on the road.

Now, only Lakha and Bilota were left.

Ting-Tong turned left and went down the street.

Bilota fired again, but yet again, Ting-Tong dodged the bullet, which hit some construction rocks instead. A rock fell on top of poor Lakha, who crashed at once. Now, only Bilota was left.

Bilota fired again, and this time, the bullet hit the car. Ting abruptly put the gear in reverse, and the car hit Bilota. There was a loud sound as the car crashed, and Ting-Tong and Ballu were thrown out.

"Haa! You thought you could get away with this. Give us that pudding," cackled Dherkhan, coming with Kallu, Lakha and Willy.

Ballu quickly jumped into the pudding, and Ting-Tong did the same. To Dherkhan's surprise, the pudding rolled into a nearby hedge.

"Bilota, you idiot, what have you done?" screamed Kallu.

Bilota got up, ran towards the hedge and fired a bullet.

There was a growling sound, and out of the hedge pounced two German Shepherds.

"How dare you shoot our farm, you interfering cat," growled the first German Shepherd.

"And what a strange shape you have?" growled the second German Shepherd.

Bilota certainly had a strange shape. He had a body the size of a basketball, a five-foot-long neck and a head the size of a cricket ball. His body also had weird colours-- half blue and half orange. All this had happened to him in an accident in a science lab. He never liked anyone to make fun of his body.

"I have a gun, and I will kill you if..." began Bilota.

But before he could continue, the German Shepherds pounced on him.

Then off went the German Shepherds to chase away Bilota.

Chapter 5
Where are Ballu and Ting-Tong?

"Phew," said Bilota, returning from his chase with the German Shepherds.

"Did anyone see Ballu?" asked Lakha.

"It's a total waste of my magic now. We won't get any animals to eat," grumbled Kallu.

"They went in that direction," said Dherkhan.

All the wild animals went where Dherkhan was pointing. It was the village market.

"Shh... everyone will get scared if they see wild animals in the village market," said Bilota. "We will have to wear these human disguises."

Soon, five weird-looking humans went into one shop. The shop woman was most astonished to see such queer creatures in her shop.

"Errr…-can I help you with anything?" she asked.

"Yes, we want a pudding. A huge pudding," answered Bilota.

"I'm sorry, this is a tailor shop. We don't have puddings here. By the way, who are you?" asked the woman.

"Oh, we are some dangerous criminals from the forest between Ballu's and Sherkhan's. By the way, do you know where the jewellery store is? We would like to rob it, and Bilota has a revolver," said stupid Lakha.

"You idiotic blabbermouth. Lakha, you will send the police after us," Bilota said, scowling at Lakha.

The shopwoman was horrified. She quickly made a dash for her smartphone and dialled the emergency number 100.

"Quick, Bilota, take out your gun and shoot her," cried Kallu.

Bilota fumbled in his pocket for his revolver. He looked up in dismay.

"It's gone. It must have fallen when the German Shepherds chased me," said Bilota.

"Then we will have to run," yelled Willy.

Suddenly, three cars came up the street with POLICE printed on them.

"The police!! Run!!!" screamed Kallu.

They all stumbled out of the shop, but unfortunately, Bilota tripped on Dherkhan's tail. And off they went, crashing down the stairs.

"To the gutter!" yelled Bilota as three policemen, including the sergeant and the inspector, hopped out of a police car.

All the animals dove into the gutter.

"Oh Bilota, why do you find such terrible hiding places, such as gutters, commodes, dustbins, coffins, graves, and coal holes," groaned Dherkhan.

Suddenly, they heard a growl in the darkness.

"Oh my god, is there another tiger down here?" said Bilota.

"No, idiot. That's my stomach growling," said Dherkhan. "I can't wait to eat those farm animals."

"Relax, we will soon eat them," replied Bilota.

They had walked about seven kilometres in the sewage pipe when Bilota opened the gutter lid and spoke.

"The coast is clear. We can resume our search now."

They got out of the gutter and entered a bookstore.

"Will you have an enormous pudding?" asked Bilota to an astonished shopman.

"Are you mad? This is a bookstore. You will find pudding in the bakery," said the man.

This was too much for Dherkhan. He threw down his disguise, pounced on the shopman, and snarled. Lakha and Willy did the same.

"Aaargghh! Tiger, Hyena and Wild Dog in my shop. Help!!!" yelled the shopman.

He dove under the chair, took out his cell phone and dialled the forest department. Dherkhan slashed at the man, and he dropped down unconscious.

"Come on," said Bilota to his team. "You are really behaving like idiots today. Let's begin our search again."

Chapter 6
A Good Long Search

They all got out of the bookstore and began to walk.

"You are all behaving like foolish idiots today! Honestly, I hope we get that pudding before sunset. What a blow it is," grumbled Bilota.

Just then, they heard a giggling sound and turned around in surprise. They saw some village children tying crackers on their tails.

Before they could do anything, one child lit the crackers.

Bang!!

"Ouch!! There is a bomb on my tail," screamed Kallu.

Bang!!

"Ow! There is a huge bomb on my tail, too!" yelled Bilota.

Frrrrrrrrrr!!

"Help!! There is a sparkler on my tail," shouted Dherkhan.

Bang! Bang! Bang! Bang! Bang! Bang! Bang!

"Help! Ouch! There are many bombs on my tail! Help!" yelped Lakha

Whoosh!

"Ouch! There is a rocket on my tail!" yelped Willy.

They walked for one or two kilometres inside the village with their burnt tails when Lakha gave a cry.

"Look there! See what I have found!"

They all looked in surprise at the direction Lakha was pointing.

"Delicious Puddings," read Bilota, "A pudding shop! We may find our pudding here. What a bit of luck! Let's go and eat all the animals now."

They all disguised themselves again and went into the pudding shop. The shopman wasn't the least surprised to see them.

"Good evening! You can choose what pudding you want here".

"Good!" said Bilota and began to search the shop with Lakha and Willy.

"Look, there are some puddings," said Lakha excitedly.

There were some strange pink, brown, black, red, white, and yellow puddings. They were kept in some small and big bowls.

"Those aren't the pudding we want," said Bilota.

"Then do we want that pudding?" pointed Willy with a grin.

Bilota looked where Willy was pointing. He gave an exclamation of delight. Behind the counter stood a shelf. On the shelf was the big bowl in which the strange pudding had been kept. But this time, the bowl was empty.

Suddenly, Kallu took out her wand and pointed it at the shop man.

"Give us that pudding right now!" she snarled in a dangerous voice.

"I won't," said the shopman and locked the strange pudding bowl in the store room.

Kallu screamed in fury and fired a curse at the man. The man dodged the curse. It hit a shelf instead, which exploded, throwing lots of puddings on the ground. The man karate-chopped Kallu on the waist, and she flew out of the shop. This was too much for Dherkhan. He threw his costume down and pounced at the man. All the customers ran out of the shop, petrified. But the shopman moved swiftly and kicked Dherkhan out of the shop. Then he kicked Lakha and Willy out of the shop, too.

Bilota saw a knife on the counter. He grabbed it and pointed it at the shopman, but the shopman boxed Bilota so hard that he flew out of the shop and landed on the other side of the street.

Bilota, Kallu, Dherkhan, Lakha and Willy searched every shop in the village, but each time, they were chased by the police or got kicked out of the shop. At last, they gave up and started walking back to the forest.

"We made such a good plan, but now it has failed," said Bilota gloomily.

Suddenly, they heard a loud beeping noise that made them nearly jump out of their skin.

Ting! Ting! Ting!

"Oh, it's my pocket Google Ball", said Kallu in surprise. "It says that something suspicious is going on in that shop over there. We must search there! Quick!"

Chapter 7
A Shock for the Enemies

They all hurried towards the shop. "It's the same pudding shop we were thrown out of a few hours ago!" said Bilota excitedly. "We shall search it thoroughly this time!"

They all got into the shop. Bilota spoke sternly to the shopman.

"We will search your shop clearly this time, and do not throw us out again."

"Oho! You, Bilota Scratchpaw, want to eat all the animals of Piggy's Farm from the strange pudding! Don't you?" said the shopman solemnly.

Bilota stared at the shopman in astonishment. How did this man know what Bilota wanted? And how did he know that his full name was Bilota Scratchpaw? Bilota looked closely at the shopman. He reminded him of someone, but he didn't know who.

Kallu suddenly took her wand out of her pocket and pointed it at the shop man.

"Tell us who you are, and how do you know so much about us?" she snarled.

"Ah, Kallu, your wand won't stop me," said the man calmly.

"I will kill you!" roared Kallu.

To their surprise, the shopman took a strange stick out of his pocket and banged it on the shop counter, murmuring something under his breath. And then, to Kallu, Bilota, Lakha and Dherkhan's amazement, all the strange little colourful puddings began to burst open, and out of them jumped Piggy, Doo, Alex, Meow, Tandoori, Ting, Tong, Naughtyhorsey, Pahari, lambs, sheep, goats, bulls, cows and hens. Then, the shopman banged his stick on himself and became Ballu!

Then they all ran out of the shop.

Kallu was so stunned that she dropped her pocket Google Ball and the magic wand. Dherkhan couldn't move a muscle due to his astonishment. Bilota, who had been knocked down by the bulls, stood up and could not believe his eyes. Lakha and Willy kept slapping each other to ensure they weren't dreaming.

Ballu turned around and fired a curse at the shop, which instantly blew up. That made all the enemies come to their senses.

"After them!" yelled Bilota.

They were soon out of the shop and running after the farm animals. Dherkhan, Lakha and Willy ran fast, followed by Kallu and Bilota. Bilota couldn't run fast because of his long neck.

Out of nowhere, two German Shepherds pounced on the road, blocking the enemies. They were the same ones who had chased Bilota.

"You!" snarled the first German Shepherd.

Suddenly, there was a burst of red light as the first German Shepherd blew up. The second German Shepherd looked around to see Kallu pointing her wand at him. With a growl of fury, he pounced on Kallu. There was a burst of red light. Kallu had killed the second German Shepherd as well.

Kallu and her troop soon caught up with the farm animals and were about to attack them when the Giggling Gang tripped them, and they fell headfirst into a pond.

"I will kill you!!!"

Bellowed Kallu as the thirteen rats giggled at her.

She took out her wand and fired a curse at the rats, who dodged it. The curse hit a car instead, which exploded. Terrified villagers ran here and there. They were out of the pond and began to chase the farm animals again, yelling at the top of their voices.

"Wait till we get hold of you!"

"We'll tear you to pieces!"

Chapter 8
What!?

Alex quickly opened the back gate of the farm and led all the farm animals in. Then, he closed the gate on the wild animals, leaving them outside.

"Let us in!" screamed Kallu, banging the gate with her fists.

But the gate was made of solid metal. Kallu had to blast it open by magic. The Farm Five ducked as the remains of the gates soared above their heads. The enemies stormed in red with anger.

"We have a surprise for you. We tricked you into going on the hunt today," chuckled Ballu.

"What!?" screamed Kallu and raised her wand to curse Ballu. But she was stopped by a sentence from Alex.

"We've had enough of your bad behaviour. You abase yourself and make everyone ashamed of you. That's why we played that trick on you," said Alex sternly.

Piggy joined him, "Oh, Kallu, you thought that you would suck all the farm animals away through your enchanted pudding and feast on us with the rest of your evil gang. But guess what? The Farm Five are never alone; we have our magician friend, Ballu, and his brave assistants, Ting and Tong. Once we solved your stupid pudding mystery, we decided to have a little fun with you."

Kallu was too angry to say anything. Willy suddenly snarled.

"It's you versus me now. I have a pack of fifty Dholes from the Pench forest, and Lakha has his cackle of fifty hyenas. You innocent farm animals won't stand a chance against me, the alpha." He growled as a hundred wild dogs and hyenas came from the forest.

"Well, we aren't just innocent animals, are we?" said Tandoori as Meow pulled his cockscomb. And he turned into a ferocious Pteranodon[1].

"We are the powerful Farm Five!" said Piggy.

He climbed a nearby hill and rolled down at full speed, knocking Willy into the jungle.

Then, Tandoori, the Pteranodon, began to attack all the wild animals. Doo began to kick them hard. Meow started to scratch them. Alex pounced on them and began to maul them. Ballu fired spells at them. Ting and Tong started

---

[1] Tandoori has a special power. When is cockscomb is pulled, he transforms into a Pteranodon and remains so for half an hour

to throw all kinds of weird stuff at the wild animals. This was too much for the dholes and hyenas, and they fled. Now, only Kallu, Bilota and Dherkhan were left. Kallu was shaking with fury.

Tandoori, the Pteranodon, swooped from the sky and took Kallu with him. He dropped her in the lake and flew back. Ballu went and hung Bilota on a tree, where he struggled in agony.

Now, only Dherkhan was left.

"I will eat you, you dumb livestock!" roared Dherkhan.

Ting-Tong came forward.

"Eat me first," Tong said eagerly.

"No, eat me first," said Ting.

"Me," said Tong.

"No, me," said Ting.

And they both began to fight. In the chaos, Dherkhan slipped and fell headfirst into Piggy's pond. When he came out, he looked exactly like a brown panther. All the farm animals burst out laughing.

"I'll teach you a lesson," he yelled.

Then he saw Gaur, Cheetal deers, Chousinga, Sambars and Chinkaras laughing at him from the jungle. A Yellow-Footed Green Pigeon fell off his perch while laughing. With a roar of embarrassment, the dark brown-coloured Tiger vanished into the jungle.

"There is only one problem left now", said Piggy, "And that is the gate". He pointed towards the gate that Kallu had blasted.

"Don't worry, the strange carpenters will fix that for you," said Ting.

Before anyone could stop them, Tong got the remains of the gate and held it upside down where it was supposed to be. Then Ting took a dart gun and fired three darts to fix the gate into the wall.

"Here is your gate," they said together.

"We want a proper gate, not a topsy-turvy one," exclaimed Alex.

"Don't worry, I will do that for you," said Ballu with a grin.

He waved his wand, and at once, the gate was alright again.

"Now it's time to go back to the jungle," said Ballu, "Come on Ting-Tong."

***

The farmer had gone to Jabalpur for some work. He was exhausted as he returned from the four-hour journey. All the animals were doing their usual work.

"What did you do when I was away?" asked the farmer.

"We solved the mystery of the Strange Pudding," said Piggy, Doo, Alex and Tandoori together.

"Well done!" said the farmer and went to the godown.

Suddenly, the kitchen door burst open, and Meow's voice came out.

"Look! I've got a new email on my Mewpad."

The four of them trooped in to see the email.

This is what it said:

Dear Farm Five,

I know that you have solved the mystery of the Strange Carpenters and the mystery of the Strange Pudding, and that is very nice.

So, I am sending you a huge pudding as a reward. It's strawberry flavour, so the colour is pink. Please share it with Naughtyhorsey, Pahari, Sheep, Hens, Goats, Cows, Bulls and Ducks.

Thanks. 😊

Regards,

Nitg Notg Allub

PS: Please do not get sucked in.

Meow tapped the screen again, and the name Nitg Notg Allub turned into Ting-Tong Ballu.

"Three cheers", said Piggy. "What a nice end to this wonderful mystery!"

Questions

Let's see how well you are reading.

1. Who sent the strange pudding?

____

2. What name did the email message come from?

    a. Wekwekpekpek

    b. Laboti Aluk

    c. kadatakagadhiginadha

3. Who was the first person the strange pudding sucked?

    a. Lamb no. 28

    b. Meow

    c. Tandoori

4. What form of transport did Ballu use to reach the farm?

a. Seaplane

b. Motorbike

c. Sleigh

5. What breed of dog chased away Bilota?

a. Tibetan Mastiff

b. Pitbull

c. German Shepard

6. What was the second shop that the wild animals visited?

a. Bookstore

b. Bakery

c. Croma

7. Who put crackers on the enemies' tails?

    a. Psychopaths

    b. Terrorists

    c. Village children

8. Who was the pudding shopkeeper?

    a. Ballu

    b. Dakia

    c. Piggy

9. Why was everyone laughing at Dherkan?

    a. He was doing Indian classical dance

    b. He fell into Piggy's pond

    c. He smashed an egg on his head

About the Author

Samay Srivastava is a young writer, storyteller, birder and naturalist. He is passionate about travelling around the world and learning different languages. He studies at the Swadhaa Waldorf School and lives in Pune with his parents.

Samay has been creating and telling stories since the age of three. At seven, he started drawing cartoon strips for his short stories, which became popular among his friends. He started writing "The Farm Five" series on his ninth birthday. His first book, "The Farm Five: The Mystery of the Strange Carpenters," was published in August 2023 and was appreciated by children and adults across the world.

Samay drives inspiration from his travels across forests and natural places in India and worldwide. His books are inspired by his safaris to Pench and Tadoba national forests. If you like this story, share your reflections at authorsamaysrivastava@gmail.com